This book belongs to

Oliver Niehaus

Best wishes from

Auntie Bon + Brian x

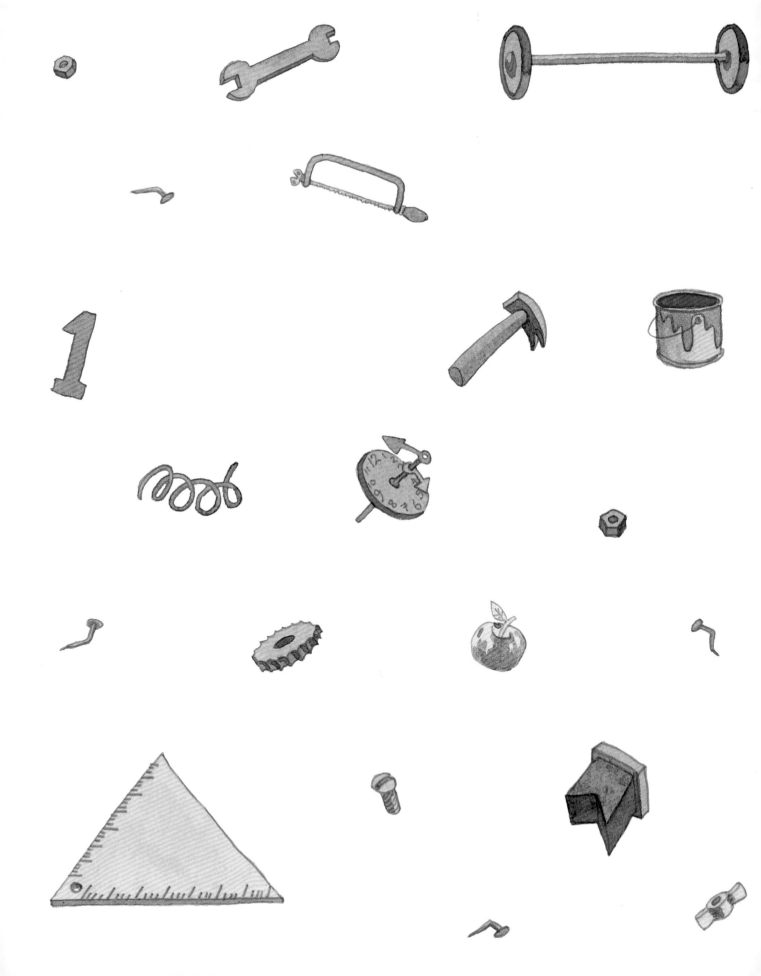

For George, with love.
A.McA.

A Gwennan Bourdon, avec amour.
S.P.

This edition first published in 2007 by Alligator Books Ltd.

cupcake

Cupcake is an imprint of Alligator Books Ltd.
Gadd House, Arcadia Avenue, London N3 2JU

Text © Angela McAllister 2003
Illustrations © Sue Porter 2003

1 3 5 7 9 10 8 6 4 2

The right of Angela McAllister and Sue Porter to be identified
as the author and illustrator of this work has been asserted by them
in accordance with the Copyright, Designs and Patents Act, 1988.
A CIP record for this title is available from the British Library.

ISBN: 978-1-84750-182-0

Printed in Malaysia

Little Jack Rabbit

written by Angela McAllister
illustrated by Sue Porter

cupcake

Jack Rabbit was visiting Grandpa in his workshop.
Grandpa could mend clocks and make dolls' houses
and even hot-air balloons.

"You are so clever," said Jack. "I wish I could be like you."

"Just watch carefully," replied Grandpa with a smile,
"and I'll teach you all I know."

But Jack wished that he could help, too . . .

Grandpa took a tape measure out of his apron pocket.

"How big am I today?" asked Jack.

"Hmm, big enough for a go-cart, I think!" said Grandpa. "Shall we get started . . ."

"Am I big enough to help, too?" asked Jack excitedly.

"No, not yet," said Grandpa. "Just watch and learn."

First they gathered the things they would need.

"But what about wheels?" asked Jack.

"Aha! Without wheels it'll be a go-nowhere-cart," Grandpa chuckled.

So they went off to the scrapyard.

They searched among pram wheels, tractor wheels and cart wheels.
At last Grandpa spotted the right ones beside a rusty old car.

"I can't squeeze through there, Jack," he said. "You'll have to reach them."
Jack climbed up beside the car. With a puff he tugged out
two large wheels and two small ones.

Back in the workshop, Grandpa began to saw the wood for the frame.
"Can I help?" asked Jack.
"I'm sorry, Jack. You're still a bit too small to use the saw,"
said Grandpa. "Just watch now and one day you'll be able to do it."

Jack Rabbit wondered if that day would ever come.
I can't do anything useful, he thought and he went outside
and kicked a fir cone around the garden.

On Grandpa's tree the
last two rosy apples were
hanging, just out of reach.
Jack climbed up to pick them.

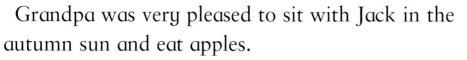

Grandpa was very pleased to sit with Jack in the
autumn sun and eat apples.

"Maybe we should just stay here all afternoon
and watch the leaves fall," he teased.

"Oh no!" cried Jack, and he tickled Grandpa
all the way back to the workshop.

The next job was to drill holes for the screws.

"Can I help?" asked Jack.

"I don't think you're big enough to use the drill, yet," said Grandpa.

As he handed Jack some screws to hold one fell and rolled under the workbench. Jack crouched down and stretched out his arm until he could almost touch the screw . . . and with one last wriggle he reached it.

"Well done!" said Grandpa. "We need that."

When the seat was fixed Grandpa fetched a pot of paint and put a big red number one on the side. "You do the other side, Jack."
Jack painted carefully but his number one wobbled.
"Don't worry," said Grandpa with a laugh, "they'll both look wobbly when you're bumping down the hill!"

At last they were ready to put on the wheels and Grandpa soon had them fixed to the frame.

"What's the rope for?" asked Jack.
"You'll need that to steer," said Grandpa. "Now your go-cart is ready to ride. We've made a beauty."

"But I didn't help at all," said Jack sadly. "I was too little."
Grandpa took off his glasses and lifted Jack
onto his knee.
"Well now," he began . . .

". . . who squeezed
through a tight space
to fetch our wheels?"
"I did," said Jack.

"Who climbed the apple
tree to pick those juicy
apples?" said Grandpa.
"I did," said Jack.

"Who reached the screw
underneath the workbench?"
said Grandpa.
    Jack began to smile.
"I did," he said.

"Who painted the
biggest number one?"
said Grandpa.
"*I did!*" said Jack.

"It seems being little is very helpful after all," said Grandpa with a grin.
"And who is going to ride this go-cart down Crooked Tree Hill?"
"You are!" said Jack.
"Oh, I can't do all the things you can do," laughed Grandpa.
"Yes you can," said Jack. "We'll do it together."
So Jack Rabbit and Grandpa pulled the go-cart to the top of Crooked Tree Hill.

Then one, two, three . . . down they raced.

Jack held on tight as Grandpa tried to steer around the
bumps but the number ones wobbled all the way.
"Again!" cried Jack happily when they had
caught their breath.

At last it was time to go home. Grandpa carried sleepy Jack.
"You know, Grandpa," said Jack, "I can do some things and
you can do some things . . . but best of all are the things we
do together."
"Quite right, Jack," chuckled Grandpa, "together, you and I
have the most wonderful times of all."